Perils of S.P.A.C.E. #4 "Return to Mechatropolis"

By

Cameron D. Blackwell

Cameron D. Blackwell

Dedicated to
David Garduno
Sami Gardner
Lisa M. Cole
Miranda Lebofsky Penner
My mom, Angel
Fans of Star Trek/Wars
Flash Gordon
Doctor Who

The Faithful Departed
John E. Sator
Santiago R. Maldonado
A. Jim Moore
Blake Beeston
Tammy Boyens
Meri Hambree

Part I: Hidden Treasure

Sundance and Timmy raced along the New Earth desert landscape in their trusty hovercar, kicking up a trail of dust behind them. Timmy carefully held three cups of coffee in his lap. They were very hot and in the process of burning his thighs something awful. Each time the car jumped, he struggled to keep everything from spilling.

"I don't see why we couldn't have gotten a cup carrier," Timmy complained. "And who drinks coffee in the desert? It just doesn't make any sense!"

"Shh, we're almost there!" Sundance accelerated the car unexpectedly, causing Timmy almost spilling the coffee for the thirtieth time. "Astralyn will be happy to see us."

"What is the deal with you two?" Timmy asked. "Ever since we got back from the Venga System, you two have been acting weird. She said something about you and some maidens..."

"I don't know what you're talking about, Timmy." Sundance did his best to avoid making any eye contact that would betray him.

"Yeah, yeah, yeah." Timmy sighed with disappointment. He had expected to get shut down.

Sundance continued to drive in silence until they reached a remote archeological dig site. They saw people gathered around a large crater that had to span for several thousand yards in diameter. At the southernmost rim, Sundance parked the car and climbed out. "Come along, Timmy."

With some creative juggling, Timmy managed to carry all of the coffee cups. He successfully climbed out of the car without spilling a drop, no thanks to Sundance.

Astralyn, wearing a pair of khaki shorts, a faded blue button-up shirt with the sleeves rolled up, and what looked like a fishing hat with misters all along the rim; all of them dirty, walked over to them and smiled.

"You found us, great job," Astralyn said. "I was afraid you'd get lost coming from Citadel City." Timmy offered her a cup of coffee. "I've got some, thanks." Timmy rolled his eyes. "Come with me. I've got something great to show you."

Astralyn led her two friends down into the crater and passed several people on their knees, picking away at the dirt. Timmy offered each of them Astralyn's coffee; they were not interested.

"A couple of days ago, one of our interns found an ancient tomb that we believe to have housed the leader of the village and their family!" Astralyn informed, positively gushing with excitement.

"I am so over tombs and temples at this point in my life," Sundance replied. "Tell me we're not going to a tomb or temple." Astralyn's intentional silence made him roll his eyes and groan.

She continued to lead them towards a large hut that was close to the rim of the crater. "We are pretty excited about this find. This could give us a glimpse into the life that existed here before the Old Earth Colonists arrived." She stopped at the hut and insisted they go inside. They reluctantly complied.

Inside was a thin man with short, spiky, blonde hair, fair skin, wearing gold-rimmed glasses, bent over in the farthest corner staring at something. He didn't acknowledge their entrance.

"Kjartan, this is Captain Sundance Starmont and Lieutenant Timmy Falken," Astralyn said.

Kjartan stood up and brushed the dirt off his knees. "Oh, Ms. Winner. I didn't hear you come in." He wiped his hands on his green button-up

4

shirt and extended his hand to Timmy. Timmy only placed Astralyn's coffee cup in it. "Thank you?"

"Don't mention it," Timmy replied.

"Did you find something?" asked Astralyn, staring into the corner.

"I think so." Kjartan stepped aside and let Astralyn access the corner. On the floor was a raised rectangular mound of dirt with a couple of pick holes in it. "As I was digging, I came upon this. I'm not one hundred percent sure, but I think it's a box."

Astralyn reached into her back pocket and pulled out a mini pick and chisel. "Let's find out, shall we?" She got on her knees and began to pick away at the dirt.

Sundance grabbed his cup of coffee from Timmy and sipped as he watched her. He didn't want to admit it, but he was intrigued.

Astralyn kept tapping away until there was a loud metallic thunk. "Kjartan, I think you might be right. Come and help me with this." Her assistant got down on his knees and helped her excavate a large silver box from its earthen prison.

"This is unlike anything we'd seen before," Astralyn noted. She gripped the box tightly as she spoke. "Everything else we found has either been bones or pottery. This is something else."

"It's a metallic box," Sundance scoffed. He took another loud sip of his coffee.

"Actually, Captain, I think it's a book," Timmy said.

Astralyn turned the box about in her hands and noticed there was a clasp keeping the metallic pages within bound. "Good eyes, Timmy." She wiped the remaining dust off of it and tried to read what was inscribed on the front. There were jagged symbols etched all over the book, nothing legible. "I can't make out what it says. Some ancient language, no doubt."

"I don't think it's human," Kjartan added. He yearned to hold the book. "May I?" Astralyn handed it to him. "I've seen something similar to this during my work as an undergrad at Citadel University. If I could see inside, I might be able to tell you more."

Kjartan tried to undo the clasp, but it refused to open.

"May I?" Sundance reached to his utility belt and pulled out his laser pistol.

"Sundance! You can't do that!" Astralyn shouted. "It's a relic of the original civilization!"

Sundance sighed and placed his gun back on his belt. He sat down next to Kjartan and examined the book. "Oh, I see it." He pressed a little silver button on the spine, and the clasp popped open. "Shooting it would have been more fun, though."

Kjartan opened the shiny book. Instantly the hut began to shake. Everyone braced themselves against a wall. The wall Astralyn was leaning on suddenly opened and revealed itself to be a door. The hut stopped shaking. Mist flowed out into the room and collected at their feet. Timmy and Sundance dropped their coffees and pulled out their pistols, waiting for something to come for them.

Part II: The First Civilization

Sundance and Timmy kept their guns aimed at the door. When nothing immediately jumped out at them, they slowly lowered them. Kjartan looked pale as he shut the book in the slim hope that the door would disappear.

"Did the book do that?" Astralyn asked. She walked over and took the book from him. He was only too happy to return it to her. She opened the book again and tried to recreate the results. Nothing happened.

"That is one scary book," Timmy said, taking a step back.

Astralyn walked back over to the door and peered inside. She whistled, and the hollow echo traveled for what sounded like forever. Her eyes lit up with joy immediately as she looked back at everyone.

"No!" Timmy and Kjartan said.

"No?" Astralyn asked incredulously. "You have to be kidding me! This is the most important discovery in the history of New Earth! We could find out who lived here before us."

"Or we could not," Timmy mumbled.

"Captain?" Astralyn turned her green eyes to Sundance for support.

"I think S.P.A.C.E. would want to take a look at it..." Sundance started, but Astralyn cut him off.

"Excellent. Kjartan, go get a light, we're going in." She ushered the poor assistant out of the hut. "This is so exciting! Boys, we're making history."

"Why do I have a feeling we're about to *be* history?" Timmy sadly mumbled.

———-

Astralyn led the way into the newly discovered cavity. With her lantern held high, she entered the cold, dark hallway. Kjartan, Sundance, and Timmy (under protest) followed closely behind. The floor was metal, so their footsteps echoed around them.

Timmy thought it was rather strange that there was so much metal inside when the outside was dirt and sand. This thought was compounded when the walls stopped, and the suspension bridge began. He gasped as he looked down and saw what seemed to be a huge spaceship in the shape of a saucer.

"Oh my goodness," Astralyn said, looking down at the cold blue ship. "Could this be a giant space saucer?" She raced down to the end of the bridge, which led inside the ship. "This is a spaceship, a really old model; probably one of the first."

"What is it doing here?" Sundance asked.

"Is it possible that the first civilization crashed here millions of years ago?" Kjartan asked, curiosity seeping into his voice. Astralyn nodded. "That would be amazing! If the bones we found are indeed human, then..."

"That could mean that Old Earth started to colonize other planets before the Space Chicken War," Astralyn added.

They stepped inside the giant spaceship. There were no lights on at all. Astralyn turned the light in the lantern up to better view the environment. The walls were metallic and had symbols matching the ones on the book. Other than that, there was nothing exceptional about the corridors.

"This reminds me of a hospital," Timmy said woefully. "I hate hospitals."

"Me too, Timmy," Sundance patted his friend on the back and pushed him forward.

Astralyn led the parade down the corridor to the left and found more of the same. They took a right turn and found themselves at a door, which was slightly ajar.

"Oh, look, a dead end." Timmy turned around and started to head back the way they came. He stopped when he realized that no one else was following him.

"Kjartan, help me with this door," Astralyn commanded.

Astralyn and Kjartan pressed themselves against the door and tried to slide it to the left. It refused to budge. Then they tried sliding it to the right. It moved an inch and then refused to move.

Sundance took out his laser pistol and shot it. Astralyn and Kjartan cursed and ducked out of the way. The door slid to the right, finally allowing them access. "I finally got to shoot something!"

"How very nice for you," Kjartan mumbled, readjusting his glasses.

Astralyn was already on the other side before Sundance could warn her to be careful. Another bridge looked down on a lot of tall, metallic silos. There were large wheels that were attached to giant gears and the like. It looked old, but only in terms of design. Everything looked brand new, devoid of dust and rust.

"What is it?" Sundance asked.

"It appears to be a processing plant of some kind," Astralyn answered. "Just look at those silos. Ingredients were stored there. I think further down is where things get processed. The people who flew this ship processed their own food while they traveled through space. Real pioneers!"

"But why live in huts?" Sundance asked.

"Maybe they lived on the ship until it could no longer provide for them." Kjartan tapped the railings of the bridge and whistled. "They had no choice but to move outside."

"I don't think that's it," Timmy said, entering the plant. "I found something."

Just then, there was a loud pop. Everyone was startled. A whirring sound started softly, then gradually grew louder. Then the wheels began to turn; slowly at first, then faster. Things below came alive with lights and hissing.

"Things are reactivating," Astralyn said, looking around. "The plant is reactivating." She could not contain her excitement.

"Guys, you really need to come and look at this," Timmy said, the urgency in his voice rising.

Sundance and the others left the plant and joined Timmy in a doorway at the other end of the corridor. Timmy only pointed inside; he didn't dare take a step inside.

Sundance walked past him and saw that there were pods lined up against all four walls. The windows were so dark he couldn't see anything inside.

"Sleeping pod," Sundance said. "But I can't see if anyone is inside it." Just as he pressed his face against the glass of a pod, a light flickered on, revealing a menacing-looking box headed robot with glaring red eyes– eyes that glared directly at him.

Part III: Escape from Mechatropolis

Sundance slowly backed away from the pod as the robot inside jerked back and forth. The one to the left of it lit up, then the one to the right of it. The pods on the south wall started to light up.

"I think now would be a good time to get out of here," Astralyn said. She and Kjartan slowly backed out of the room. Timmy was right behind them.

All of the robots were reactivating and climbing out of the pods. Timmy and Sundance took out their laser pistols and took off running down the corridor. The robots immediately ran after them with surprising speed. Sundance and Timmy turned around and shot at the robots with fantastic accuracy. The robots slowed down in their pursuit of them but were not deterred.

"Captain!" Timmy called Sundance's attention to the fact that more robots were joining the chase. "There's too many of them! We can't fight them all off!"

"Just keep shooting!" Sundance commanded.

Astralyn and Kjartan led the way through the corridors, trying to remember which way they came. Astralyn knew they didn't take too many turns, but even the simplest of directions under pressure could quickly turn complicated.

They stopped at a four-way intersection. "I don't remember being here," Astralyn said. "None of this looks familiar."

"All the walls look the same," Kjartan added. "I knew we should have brought some bread crumbs! I even had a sandwich for lunch."

"Not helping," Astralyn mumbled.

Sundance and Timmy, who were bringing up the rear, caught up with Astralyn and Kjartan. "Why has the running stopped?" Sundance demanded. "Must go faster!"

Astralyn didn't want to tell him that she didn't know where they were. She looked at all three directions and took a deep breath. Let's try forward, she thought. She ran straight ahead, and the group followed.

The short pause allowed the robots to gain some space. They reached out their arms for them, yearning to touch them. As Sundance continued to pummel the robots with laser beams, he took time to realize that they had mouths. Before he could question why they had mouths, he saw that when they opened, there were rows of sharp metallic teeth. *Why in the world would robots need teeth?*

Sundance thought. *Just keep shooting them, and hopefully, we won't need to find out.*

Timmy and Sundance continued to fire at the robots, but they seemed to be impervious. Sundance tried shooting the first line of robots in their eyes, but the robots kept coming. There didn't seem to be any weak spots.

"Oh, come on!" Sundance shouted.

After a right turn, the group was relieved to find the bridge leading to the outside world. As they ran, the bridge trembled with each footstep. Astralyn thought it was because of everyone's combined weight, but as she neared the end, she realized the bridge was withdrawing back inside the ship.

"Hurry up," Astralyn shouted. "The bridge!"

The others already knew. Astralyn was the first to leap from the bridge to the sandy floor of the hut. The gap between wasn't that wide. Kjartan had to jump a little further, but he managed.

Sundance and Timmy were still walking backward, shooting at the quickly approaching robots. They seemed to be walking in place, like a metallic treadmill. The gap was growing wider.

"Timmy, go ahead and jump," Sundance commanded. "I'll be right there."

Timmy wanted to argue, but he knew that there was no time. He placed his laser pistol in his belt and turned to jump. He made the mistake of looking down into the black abyss below.

"Timmy, hurry!" Astralyn said. She held out her hands as Timmy made the jump. She caught him and pulled him onto the ledge. "Sundance!"

The robots were now on the bridge with Sundance. No matter how many laser blasts he fired off, they kept coming! There was no point in firing anymore. He placed his pistol on his hip and turned around to make the jump; only the gap was widening at an alarming rate.

"Captain, come on!" Timmy called. "We'll catch you!"

Sundance didn't like the sound of that but knew he had no choice. He took a deep breath and jumped from the bridge. It was mid-jump he realized that he was going to come up short of the ledge. He was going to fall to his death in the abyss below. The edge of the spaceship, assuming it was saucer-shaped, would catch him and break his fall.

"Kjartan! Timmy!" Without having to be told, they quickly linked elbows as Astralyn leaned out into the gap. She reached out her free hand and with surprising strength, caught Sundance. "Don't let go!" she commanded.

Kjartan and Timmy pulled Astralyn and Sundance back into the hut. They collapsed in a heaping, panting pile, thankful to be alive.

Kjartan was the first to sit up. "We're not out of the woods yet." They all sat up and saw that the bridge was no longer retreating. Once they learned that their prey had escaped, they flipped a switch, and now the bridge was extending towards them.

"The door!" Sundance shouted.

They all got up and ran to the open door. Despite all four of them pushing it, the door did not want to move.

"Push!" Sundance commanded.

"What do you think we're doing?" Astralyn replied.

"A little help!" Kjartan called out.

The other archeologists ran into the hut and immediately knew what to do. With their combined strength, they were able to shut the door. The robots pounded on the door, demanding to be free. Sundance leaned with his back against the door and wiped his brow.

"Humans 1, robots 0," he said.

As if on cue, the entire hut began to quake. The ceiling cracked and threatened to come down. Everyone ran outside just in time for it all to collapse into a pile of dirt. It was then that the entire crater started to shake. Something bigger was coming for them.

Part IV: What Lies Beneath

Panic set in as the entire crater began to quake violently. People ran for their lives in all directions. Astralyn, Kjartan, Sundance, and Timmy stood and watched as the ground cracked open.

"Everyone out of the crater!" Sundance commanded. They didn't need to be told twice. People sprinted to the nearest declared exits in an unorderly fashion.

"What is going on?" Kjartan asked.

"I think they're leaving," Sundance replied.

The shaking became more intense. Pieces of the ground gave way as the cracks grew wider. A low humming noise joined the chaos. The sound caused the ground to vibrate more than it already had been. Before it had been sinking, now the ground was starting to rise.

"Oh my god," Astralyn gasped.

"To the car, to the car!" Sundance shouted.

Everyone that had a vehicle hopped in it and quickly sped away. Kjartan and Astralyn jumped into the back seats of Sundance's car.

"Everyone buckle up!" Sundance started the car as he hopped in it. Timmy climbed in and buckled his seat belt. Astralyn and Kjartan did the same.

The hovercar lifted off the unsteady ground and flew off into the distance. The ground continued to rise to meet them. At one point, the ground threatened to come crashing down on them as it crested into a massive wave. The humming grew even louder. The hovercar drove as fast as it could, but it didn't seem to be fast enough.

Astralyn covered her ears as the wind whipped past them. She looked back and saw that the spaceship was rising out of the crater. It spun around, sending the dirt that had once rested on it flying everywhere.

"Oh my god," she whispered again.

When the spinning saucer was finally free of the ground, it hovered over the fleeing humans for a moment and then flew off into space.

Sundance and Timmy could see that S.P.A.C.E. Headquarters had already begun firing at the ship, but its shields protected it from getting damaged. Sundance didn't care if the robots were destroyed; he was just glad they were leaving. He stopped the car and let it hover in neutral.

"Is everyone okay?" Sundance looked back at Astralyn and Kjartan. Both of them looked shocked beyond reason. "I'll take that as a yes. Let's go home, people."

———

"Just what the hell was that?" Admiral Graves sat down at his desk. Sundance and Timmy thought it best to check in with him as soon as they got back to base. "One minute, it's peaceful, and then the next, there's an earthquake!"

"Astralyn and one of her assistants stumbled upon a book..." Sundance tried to explain.

"A book?"

"Well, it looked like a book, but it opened a door in the hut that led to a giant space saucer that was trapped underground," Sundance spoke as quickly as he could to prevent the admiral from interrupting again. "I pushed the button to the book, and that's what started everything. The ship came back to life. Then the carnivorous robots woke up and tried to eat us, sir."

"Carnivorous robots?"

"They had huge teeth, sir."

Sundance and Timmy saw that the admiral was having a hard time with the scenario. There wasn't anything they could say that would make it any more believable.

"You mean to tell me that there was a ship full of sleeping carnivorous robots underneath Citadel City for years, and no one knew about it?"

"Well, the previous civilization might have known about it, sir," Timmy said. "But they didn't leave any notes behind."

"Well, they're gone now, right?" Admiral Graves asked.

"I believe so," Sundance replied.

"Good riddance. Now I have to calm the citizens down and assure them that the worst is over." The admiral stood up and dismissed Sundance and Timmy.

As they left the admiral's office, Timmy felt a knot developing in the pit of his stomach. He tried to attribute it to all the excitement that happened earlier, but he knew better.

———

Later that night at the New Earth Museum of Artifacts, Kjartan sat alone in Astralyn's office, staring at a black backpack. He had been sitting there for twenty minutes staring at it, willing himself just to open it.

"Man up, Kjartan!" He took a deep breath and reached for the bag. He punched in a four-digit code on the lock, and the backpack opened. He reached inside and pulled out the metallic book. He dropped it on the table and stared at it for a moment. He couldn't believe it was really there. It shouldn't be there, but he couldn't live with the idea of abandoning it in the ruins. He believed Astralyn was right when she said it was possibly the greatest discovery. It deserved to be explored.

Finding his courage, he held his breath as he pressed the button on the spine. The book immediately popped open. With great care, he flipped open the first page. He examined the writing inside and instantly felt he recognized it.

He jumped up from his desk and ran to the bookcase. After excitedly searching the shelves, he found the book he was looking for, sat down, and scoured both books for a translation. The first word he translated was 'Mechanomitron.' He took out a notepad and started taking notes.

An hour later, Kjartan had finished going through the books. He got on the phone and called Astralyn.

"Ms. Winner, you have to come to the museum and see this!" He hung up the phone and waited. Twenty minutes later, Astralyn strolled into the office. She gasped when she saw the Mechanomitron sitting on her desk.

"Kjartan, you didn't..."

"I did! You were right; there were people on this planet before us." Kjartan stood up from his seat and pushed Astralyn towards the book. "The robots brought them here. They used this planet like a farm. They would bring humans here, let them flourish, then come back and harvest them. They'd leave a few behind so that they would repopulate, then go to another planet to harvest humans there!"

"The robots must have crashed here on their way back to harvest and couldn't get free," Astralyn whispered. "Until today."

Astralyn noticed that a little red light on the book had been flashing on and off on its spine. "How long has it been doing that?" she asked.

Kjartan picked up the book and looked at the spine. "I don't know."

Astralyn knew that this was not good news. "They're coming back."

Part V: Robots of Menace

In the war room, Ensign Harriman sat at his console, monitoring the satellite system in space. It was supposed to be a routine shift. He and his coworkers usually sat at their desks drinking tea, coffee, even hot chocolate on occasion while they read the paper, played word games, or watched old TV shows from Old Earth, nothing too exciting. With Captain Sundance running around pissing off Space Chickens with giant spaceships, things had become more exciting than he could bear. The giant spaceship this morning got everyone upset. The thought of a spaceship full of homicidal robots in their backyard was terrifying. Ensign Harriman just hoped for a quiet evening.

"Ensign Harriman, I'm picking up something on long-range scanners," said a crewman. "Putting it on screen now."

"No, no, no!" Ensign Harriman muttered under his breath.

On the large viewscreen, an image of a giant saucer appeared. Ensign Harriman recognized it as the one from earlier. He immediately picked up the phone and dialed a number. "Admiral, you need to see this."

Before Harriman hung up the phone, the admiral walked in and sat down in his chair.

"That thing again, eh?" Graves said, shifting the cushion of his seat. "Fire lasers!"

Ensign Harriman pressed a few buttons, and the lasers fired. On the screen, they were able to see that the robots' shields kicked in and stopped the lasers before impact.

"How is that possible? It's older than dirt!" Admiral Graves ordered another shot, but it yielded the same result. "What's the point of having a satellite laser system if everything is impervious to it?"

The spaceship flew right through the satellite defense and headed towards the S.P.A.C.E. Headquarters. It hovered overhead for a few minutes. People all over Citadel City looked up into the night sky and saw the saucer hovering there. They screamed when they saw robots were rappelling down from their ship.

The robots landed all over the city and started to round people up. When they caught them, they activated their jetpacks and flew back up to the ship.

"All S.P.A.C.E. agents, please report for duty," the admiral said over the loudspeaker. All the agents gathered and immediately left to fight the robots.

Sundance and Timmy arrived at the scene downtown and shot at a group of robots that were trying to corner a lovely couple trying to enjoy a night out.

"You there, robots!" Sundance called out as he hopped out of his hovercar. "You leave those men alone!" He and Timmy fired at them. The robots were distracted long enough to allow the couple to escape. The lasers bounced off the robots' chests.

"They still aren't working!" Timmy exclaimed. "What kind of robots are these?"

"I don't know, Timmy, but just keep firing!"

The robots lost interest in them and walked away.

"Hey! I'm shooting you! Pay attention to me!" Sundance shouted.

"Man, who knew going to visit Astralyn would result in mass chaos?" Timmy asked, shooting at the now retreating robots.

"I should have known," Sundance mumbled. Then he slapped his forehead. "Astralyn! Timmy, get in the car!" He ran back to the car and started it up. Timmy was barely able to hop in the car before Sundance sped off.

"Where are we going?" Timmy asked. He looked behind them and saw that other S.P.A.C.E. agents were taking care of the robots they left behind. "What about the robots?"

"Do you ever stop asking questions?" Sundance replied. "We're going to check on Astralyn. If the robots returned, I bet it has something to do with that book."

———

Astralyn and Kjartan heard the sound of the giant space saucer hovering above the museum and instantly shut the metallic book.

"Make it stop blinking," Kjartan said, pushing the book in Astralyn's direction.

"What makes you think I know anything about how this book works?" Astralyn replied. She pushed it back in Kjartan's direction. "You opened it; you figure it out!"

"I'm just an intern!"

A loud thump sounded from above. *Was someone on the roof?* Astralyn looked out the window and saw robots floating down from the sky. They were massing in front of the museum. One of them looked her way. She gasped and shut the curtain.

"They know we're here," Astralyn said. Kjartan was still looking at the blinking light and silently panicking. "We need to either get out of here or hide."

"Maybe if we just give them the book, they'll take it and leave us alone."

"They're a group of nomadic, carnivorous robots," Astralyn said. "I don't think they're just going to call it a day. Come on!"

Astralyn grabbed Kjartan and pulled him out of the office. They traveled in the shadows to the back of the building. They stopped when they heard thumping and then a buzzing noise on the roof.

"What is that?" Kjartan asked.

"It's our cue to shut up and hide." Astralyn led them to the basement near the back of the building. There was a code needed to open the door. She punched a five-digit passcode, and the door clicked open. She pushed Kjartan inside and shut the door behind her.

Kjartan turned on a light, but Astralyn quickly turned it off. "No lights!"

They sat in the dark and listened to the sounds of the robots breaking into the museum. Astralyn tried not to think about the amount of cleanup and paperwork she'd have to do after this adventure.

Astralyn backed away from the door and stared at the thin slice of light at the bottom. The light shifted as the robots' feet shuffled outside the door. She and Kjartan jumped as the door knob jiggled slowly. Though the handle made a full rotation, the door remained closed. Everything went quiet. Astralyn continued to hold her breath. Did they get bored and leave? Astralyn checked the bottom of the door and found it to be clear of obstructions. Kjartan and Astralyn let out a collective sigh. Then a fist punched through the door.

Part VI: Into the Lions' Den

As Sundance and Timmy arrived at the museum, they noticed there was a large group of robots assembled in the front. "We're too late," Sundance said.

"Again," Timmy added.

The robots turned around in unison and stared at them with their glowing red eyes. This sent shivers down Timmy's spine. They all slowly marched towards them. Knowing that they weren't going to do any damage to them, Sundance took out his laser pistol and began firing at them.

"Stupid robots think they're better than us," Sundance said. "Hold on!" He revved the engine of his hovercar and took off at breakneck speed. "If this doesn't stop them, nothing will."

He steered directly towards the robots and knocked them over. Robots went flying left and right. When he reached the steps of the museum, Sundance turned the car around and plowed through the remaining robots. The courtyard was full of dented and prone robots. He stopped the car and let it settle to the ground.

"Be impervious to that!" Sundance shouted triumphantly.

Suddenly, there was a scream from up above. Timmy and Sundance looked up and saw that two robots were flying up towards the mother ship with Astralyn and Kjartan in tow.

"Astralyn!" Sundance called out. "They've taken Astralyn!"

"Again," Timmy added.

Sundance jumped out of the car and ran to one of the damaged robots. He saw they had jet packs strapped to them. He didn't question why the robots had jet packs; he just knew that he could use them.

"Timmy, come and help me get the jetpack off this robot," Sundance commanded.

"Why does it have a jetpack?" Timmy got out of the car and helped Sundance roll the robot over.

Sundance retrieved the jet pack and promptly started putting it on. Once he was buckled in, he started the engine.

"Wait for me," Timmy said. He quickly started to look for a jet pack as well.

"No, Timmy." Sundance placed his right hand on Timmy's left shoulder and shook his head. "I need you to get back to headquarters."

"I can do this!"

"I know you can, but I need you to help come up with something that will stop these robots." Sundance looked up at the space saucer and sighed. More robots were flying back up there with people in tow. "I need to go up there and save those people. When you've got something, let me know!"

"I'll do my best, Captain." Timmy saluted him. "Good luck, sir."

Sundance nodded his head. He pressed a button and flew into the sky.

Timmy looked at the metallic carnage and sighed. Some of the robots sparked and twitched. With each pop, Timmy jumped. "Screw this noise." He hopped into Sundance's car and drove back to headquarters.

————

Sundance arrived at the docking bay of the robot's spaceship. He was more than a little irritated that he was back on the ship. He turned off the jet pack and threw it on the ground. He quickly scanned the area and found a pillar to hide behind. As he hid, another stream of robots with a fresh batch of humans flew in. They screamed as the robots led them towards their doom.

Sundance carefully peered out from behind the pillar and watched as the robots ushered the humans into a holding room. Once they were safely deposited, the robots locked them inside and walked further down the corridor. He waited for a few minutes before he dared to come out into the open.

He tiptoed over to the holding room and knocked on it. People inside shouted for help. He quickly shushed them and told them to be quiet. "I'm going to get you out of there. Stand back." He heard them take his advice. He took out his trusty laser pistol and aimed it at the locking mechanism. The lock sparked, and the door opened.

People quickly ran out and pushed him aside. They ran back to the docking bay and stopped when they realized that they couldn't go anywhere. With no other jet packs to use, the forty-plus people were stuck on the ship.

Astralyn and Kjartan approached Sundance. Kjartan looked grateful, but Astralyn looked irritated. "So what's the plan?" she asked.

"To tell you the truth, I didn't really think that far ahead," Sundance admitted. "I just wanted to get you out of there."

"Well, thank you, but next time..." Astralyn started.

"I'll just leave your butt up here." Sundance smirked at her.

"I really hope you didn't set off an alarm or something," Kjartan said.

Suddenly, a klaxon sounded. Astralyn and Sundance turned and glared at Kjartan.

"What? I didn't do it!" Kjartan put his hands up in the air.

"So what now, O fearless leader?" Astralyn asked sarcastically.

Sundance didn't know what to do. He thought about asking everyone to get back in the room, but then what? Maybe he should have stayed with Timmy. He was just so focused on saving Astralyn. He never said that planning was his strong suit.

"Sundance!" Astralyn snapped him back into the moment.

"Hold on, I'll think of something!" Sundance could hear the sound of the robotic footsteps approaching. He needed to act fast. He scanned the bay and saw that there wasn't anything that he could use as a weapon, not offhand. The only thing he had was his laser pistol. That wasn't going to cut the mustard. At this moment, he wished he had thought this out more.

"We need to get back in the room," Sundance said. "Everyone, back into the room." The people protested. "Or would you rather jump?"

The people mulled it over. "Just get into the room!"
The people reluctantly agreed and walked back
towards the holding room.

Ten robots arrived too quickly and blocked
their approach, gnashing their teeth, arms
outstretched. Sundance ran to the front of the
crowd and pulled out his laser pistol, ready to
defend. He fired a few warning shots, but the
robots kept coming. With each menacing step
forward, the people would take a step backward.
This continued until they reached the open door,
with only open air and the ground below. Sundance
knew that he had run out of time. There was
nothing left to do but surrender.

Part VII: Blasted

Timmy managed to make his way safely from the museum to S.P.A.C.E. Headquarters. He ran down the halls until he reached the Research and Development laboratories. He slammed open the doors and stood in the doorway panting. The two researchers in the lab were startled, almost dropping the beakers of fluid they were holding.

"Help," Timmy gasped. "I need help!"

Dr. Rothery ran to him and escorted him to a seat. "Are you alright, sir?" she asked.

"There are giant man-eating robots on the loose; of course I'm not alright!" The other researcher, Dr. MacFadden, gave Timmy a glass of water, which he quickly drank. "I need something..." He took another deep breath and tried again. "I need something that will defeat the killer robots. The laser pistols aren't working."

Dr. Rothery looked confused. "There are killer robots outside? Why doesn't anyone tell us these things?"

"I think the admiral made an announcement," Dr. MacFadden said, rubbing his hands together. He walked over to his desk and rifled through a stack of papers, many of them doodles and blueprints. "I think I was working on something in case of a giant robot invasion over here last week."

"Really?" Timmy asked.

"Well, you want to be prepared for anything."

Dr. Rothery joined the search. "Reptilian attacks? No. Amphibian attacks... Oh, here's the Space Chicken attack. I guess we're a little late on that." She grabbed another sheet of paper. "Ah-ha! Robot invasion attack."

"It's always in the last place you look," Dr. MacFadden said.

"Of course it is," Rothery replied matter-of-factly. She brought the blueprint over to Timmy and let him take a look at it. "In theory, this weapon should allow the user to create an electromagnetic blast which should disable any mechanoid. We called it the 'Electromagnetic Blaster.' Catchy, isn't it?"

"In theory?" Timmy asked. "Nevermind. It sounds great. How soon and how fast can you make this thing?"

"Oh, it's already done." Dr. MacFadden pointed to a cabinet where they kept all of their prototypes. Timmy stood up and walked over to it. When he opened it, he saw many gadgets and gizmos. He immediately found the weapon.

"Is this a modified shotgun?" Timmy pulled the gun out of the cabinet and tested its weight. The doctors nodded. "Nice. Thanks a lot, you guys!"

Timmy ran out of the lab. The doctors tried to warn him that it hadn't been tested and that they weren't even sure it had a power supply in it, but they figured he'd find out soon enough.

———

Timmy ran out of the headquarters and back into the chaos and mayhem happening outside. He saw some robots ganging up on a few S.P.A.C.E. agents and thought it would be the perfect time to try the weapon out. He confidently cocked the shotgun and pulled the trigger. A big blue wave of energy flew out of the barrels and hit the robots. They froze in place for a moment and then sparks spewed from their bodies. They collapsed to the ground and twitched.

"Bullseye!" Timmy said.

The S.P.A.C.E. agents thanked him and commented on his new toy. They asked if he had any more.

"Ask Dr. Rothery and MacFadden," Timmy replied. "In the meantime, I have a date with a couple of robots."

He walked over to one of the defunct robots and stole its jetpack. It wasn't using it anymore.

―――――――

Sundance watched as the robots herded the people out of the docking bay and towards the processing plant in a single file line. He maneuvered himself to the back of the line while he tried to come up with a plan. He felt frustrated for not having done so earlier. He couldn't let the robots process those people into food. He frantically looked around him to see if there was anything he could use to fight off the robots. Underneath the jetpack he had just used, there was a long metal pipe lying there.

"How convenient," he said aloud.

He picked up the pipe and examined it. He supposed it would have to do. He was about to head back down the hallway when he stopped and looked back at the jetpack. "Hmmm..."

―――――――

"Do you think he's just gonna leave us here?" Kjartan asked. A robot prodded him with a staff to move him towards the processing plant.

"He's not going to leave us to die, Kjartan," Astralyn replied. "That's not his style. I don't know what plan he's got, but I sure hope it's a good one." She looked ahead and saw the processing plant was just around the corner to the right. She hoped Sundance would arrive soon.

A few minutes later, they reached the processing plant. The smell of oil and steam filled the room. The heat was oppressive. They crossed a bridge and then followed the stairs down to the lower level.

There were robots lined up against the walls, making sure no one stepped out of line. She looked at Kjartan and saw that he was thinking about running away. She shook her head, indicating that he wouldn't make it very far before they caught him. He sighed and kept walking.

"Everybody run!" Sundance's voice came from above them. Everyone looked up and saw that he was flying around using a jetpack. As soon as he swooped down, the people quickly dispersed throughout the plant.

The robots raised their arms and fired lasers at the fleeing people and up at Sundance. The captain deftly maneuvered past the laser beams and swung the pipe, breaking their lasers. He zipped back up again to get out of their reach.

"How do you like them apples?" Sundance gloated.

More robots entered the plant from the entrance above and shot Sundance's jetpack, setting it on fire and rendering it useless. He immediately fell to the floor with a thud. The robots swiftly gathered around him. All Sundance could see were their evil red eyes staring down at him.

Part VIII: Timmy the Robot Slayer

Two of the menacing robots reached down and pulled Sundance to his feet. They stripped him of the jetpack and threw it away. Sundance was too sore to fight back. He looked up, defeated, and saw that the robots had found the others. They rounded them up and made them line up in a single file. His robot captors pushed him into the line, conveniently next to Astralyn and Kjartan.

"That was a brilliant plan," Astralyn said, rolling her eyes.

"It worked for a little bit, didn't it?" Sundance shook his head and sighed. "It should have worked. There were more robots that I realized."

"I was rooting for you," Kjartan said. He patted Sundance on the back.

"At least some people are appreciative," Sundance said.

The line marched tragically forward. Sundance dared to step out of the line to see where the line was headed. The people at the front of the line were climbing a flight of stairs connected to one of the large silver silos.

"Looks like we're going back upstairs," Astralyn said.

"What do you think they're going to do to us?" Kjartan asked.

"They're probably going to make us fall into that silo, which will have a device that will either mash us or grind into a gooey paste," Sundance answered candidly. Kjartan whimpered.

"Do you have any more bright ideas?" Astralyn asked.

"Timmy."

———

Timmy flew up into the docking bay with the Electromagnetic Blaster primed and ready. When he saw that there wasn't anyone there, he landed. He quietly took off his jetpack and tiptoed down the corridors. He carefully peered around corners to see if any robots were nearby. They were eerily empty, just the way he wanted it.

Timmy heard the loud whirring noises of the processing plant and knew where he needed to go. As he neared the plant, he began to see more robots headed in the area. He likened it to people hanging out in the kitchen when food is ready to be served.

The plant was right around the corner. Four robots were guarding the door. Timmy sighed and said, "This is it." He jumped out into the corridor and blasted two of the robots dead. They fell to the floor and exploded. Before the other two robots could figure out what had happened, Timmy blasted them. They exploded seconds later. Steaming robot chunks were everywhere.

"Cool beans," Timmy said.

He stepped over the remains and entered the plant. The three robots at the end of the bridge were startled, but he quickly shot them. More explosions.

By this time, the robots on the floor noticed that their brethren had just been killed. They all turned their attention away from the line and focused on Timmy, firing their lasers. Timmy ducked and dodged each laser while blasting the robots on his way down the stairs.

Sundance saw this and shouted, "NOW!" He immediately rushed the robots monitoring the line. The people followed suit and toppled over their oppressors. Some of the robots even tried to run away, but the people tackled them to the floor.

When Timmy reached the end of the stairs, he tucked and rolled off of them and shot two robots that were coming his way. They collided into each other and exploded. He ran over and helped the people take down more robots.

"Timmy, you did it!" Sundance said. "I knew you could do it!"

"Thanks, Captain," Timmy said. "You should really thank Doctors Rothery and MacFadden. They came up with…"

"Timmy, behind you!" Astralyn shouted.

Without even looking, Timmy fired a shot over his shoulder. The robot that was sneaking up on him exploded instantly. He looked heroic as his silhouette stood out against the fiery backdrop of the explosion.

Timmy looked around and found that most of the robots had been destroyed. "I love this thing!"

"What we need to do now is to stop the processing plant," Sundance said. "And I know just how to do it. Timmy, we need to find the bridge."

"I got it!" Timmy said. "Stop the ship, stop the plant."

"And don't forget about the robots on the ground," Astralyn reminded.

"You and your intern help the people jet pack it out of here," Sundance commanded. "Timmy and I will stop the ship."

"Aye aye, captain." Astralyn mock saluted him before she and Kjartan left to follow his orders.

Timmy and Sundance ran up the stairs and across the bridge to arrive at the entrance to the plant. Timmy led them down several corridors, blasting robots as they came.

It took them a while, but they finally made it to the bridge. Timmy wiped out all of the robots that were there. When the smoke cleared, Timmy and Sundance tiptoed through the remains to reach the weapons console.

"Can you patch that weapon into the ship's weapons system?" Sundance asked.

"Can I? How is that even a question?" Timmy immediately went to work. He crawled underneath the panel, pulled out some wires, and attached them to the blaster. He typed in a few commands, and the blaster was ready. "When I press the button, the blaster will send the command to..."

"Great!" Sundance pressed the button, and the ship emitted a tremendous amount of energy. Like a tsunami wave, the electromagnetic pulse swept across the land below and ravaged the robots. On the ground, robots everywhere shorted out and then exploded into a million fiery pieces. The people cheered and celebrated.

"Uh, oh," Timmy said.

"Uh, oh? What uh, oh?"

In response, all of the systems on the ship powered down at the same time. Timmy looked at Sundance and smiled weakly. "I forgot that the ship would be affected as well."

"That's not good." Sundance scrambled to the navigation control panel to see if he could turn it back on somehow, but it was dead. The pulse had knocked it out of commission. There was nothing left to do but let the ship crash to the ground.

Part IX: Crash and Burn

"Timmy, I need something! I'll take any power you can give me!" Sundance tapped on the navigation console in the hopes that it would come alive.

Timmy looked around and couldn't find anything right away. "Umm... umm..." He looked at the Electromagnetic Blaster. If it worked once... He disconnected the blaster from the weapons console and moved it over to the navigation console. He reached down and pulled a few errant wires from it and wrapped it around the blaster.

"I don't know if this is going to work," Timmy said as the ship took a drastic nosedive. "Here goes nothing." He pressed a button on the console, but nothing happened. He tried it again, but the result was the same.

"But it worked the first time," Sundance said.

"All the systems were on the first time," Timmy replied. "We fried everything with the electromagnetic pulse."

Sundance slammed his fist on the console. "Dammit! We go through all this trouble to save these people only to put them right back in harm's way." Timmy gave it a quick tap before Sundance slammed on it one more time, and then the console came alive.

"Captain, you did it!" Timmy patted Sundance on the back. "You made it work again."

"All it needed was to know who it was working for," Sundance said, reveling in the moment. "Let's see if I can make this baby fly!"

He pushed a button on the console, and a little screen popped up with the robotic language displayed on it. He couldn't make out what it was saying, but he had a pretty good idea. Piloting consoles hadn't changed much throughout the ages. While this flying saucer was an old model, the basics were still the same– he hoped.

"Hold onto your butts," Sundance said.

He took the controls and tried his best to keep the ship from crashing into Citadel City. The ship shook with extreme violence as it slowly soared over the city. He felt the front of the saucer dip lower just as they reached the border, threatening to take out a tall building. The ship passed without incident.

The console started to blink on and off. "Timmy, what does that mean?" He knew what it meant.

"The console is losing power, Captain," Timmy confirmed.

"Wire the weapon now!"

"It's already wired, sir. We're draining the weapon." Timmy picked up the blaster and sighed. "It wasn't meant to power an entire ship!"

"Fine, I'll see if I can set her down gently."

Sundance strained to retain control of the ship. As soon as it was safely away from Citadel City, Sundance looked for a suitable place to crash. He spotted the area the ship had lain dormant for centuries.

"The crater," Timmy said. "That's brilliant!"

"You're just saying that." Sundance winked at Timmy as he piloted the ship towards the crater.

The console stopped blinking, and the display slowly faded away. There was no more power. Sundance stepped away from the controls and threw his hands in the air.

"That's all I got," he said. "Let's get out of here and hope Astralyn was able to get most of those people out of here." He turned around and left the bridge. Timmy picked up the blaster, unraveled the wires, and then followed Sundance out.

They ran down the corridors to the best of their ability, with the ship continuing on its nosedive. It threatened to make them walk on the ceiling. With strong determination, they raced down the corridors until they reached the docking bay. Astralyn and Kjartan were waiting for them.

"It's about time," Astralyn said. She handed the boys jetpacks; then, she put on her own. "I thought the captain always went down with the ship."

"It depends on whose ship it is," Sundance said, smirking at her. Astralyn looked disgusted.

They all jumped out of the docking bay and used the jet packs to get as far away from the crashing ship as possible. When they were a safe distance away, they watched the saucer crash back into the crater it had previously occupied. There was a large explosion, which sent debris flying everywhere.

Sundance, Kjartan, Astralyn, and Timmy piloted their jet packs back to Citadel City, not wanting to have anything more to do with the remains.

———

"Is it really over this time?" Admiral Graves sat in his chair in the war room. Astralyn, Kjartan, Sundance, and Timmy all stood beside him, looking at the viewscreen. The image of the destruction of the ship was haunting to see. "Are those suckers really dead?"

"I believe them to be so, Admiral," Sundance reported.

"And what about that book?" Admiral Graves looked at Kjartan and Astralyn.

"If it was on that ship, it's been obliterated," Astralyn replied. She looked over at Kjartan, and he nodded at her.

"If?" The admiral did not look pleased.

"It was on the ship, sir," Astralyn amended.

"Good!" Admiral Graves stood up from his chair and smiled. "Then I can take a piss. I've been holding it all day! Astralyn, always a pleasure. Gentlemen." He swiftly exited the war room. "Try not to resurrect anything while I'm gone."

Kjartan let out a sigh of relief as the admiral walked past him. "You don't have to tell me twice. At first, I was happy to go out in the field, but now? I'm never leaving the office again. You can count on that!"

"It all comes with the territory if you hang around Sundance long enough," Astralyn joked.

"No offense, Captain, but I hope I never see you around the office. Good day." Kjartan half-heartedly saluted Sundance and Timmy and found his way out of the war room.

"Say, let's all go get some dinner!" Sundance said.

"Are you buying?" Timmy asked.

"I think dinner will be on the museum tonight." Astralyn fished a green credit card out of her pocket. Sundance and Timmy cheered as the three of them left the war room.

———

At the crater, S.P.A.C.E. agents were combing the area for all the pieces of scrap metal. Anything and everything was picked up, that was if it wasn't on fire.

"I don't see why we always have to clean stuff like this up," complained one worker.

"Because it's our job!" replied another worker.

They both walked by a piece of metal that once belonged to a robot. When they had gotten far enough away, a little red light began to flash off and on.

The End

Next Time On Perils of S.P.A.C.E.:

A malevolent computer virus takes over a space station intent on destroying New Earth. The crew of the StarTango must do battle with an ever-evolving evil in "Mission: Theta."

Made in the USA
Las Vegas, NV
22 January 2021